WHAT'S THE MATTER, MR. GIRAFFE?

By Gloria Menifield

First U.S. edition 2002

Library of Congress Control Number: 2002103428

ISBN: 0-9716442-1-7

All rights reserved. Published by Jackson Publishing
Southaven, MS 38672

Printed in Hong Kong

Dedicated to Mrs. Young's 2001-2002 Kindergarten Class
Hernando Elementary
Hernando, Mississippi

Visit us online at www.jacksonbooks.com.

Oh no! Could it be,
is it rain that I see?

Must be, Must be,
because I also see,
big drops, little drops,
going flop, flop, flop.

We must go, so we don't get wet.

I must admit the last time
we got wet, it was a mess.
You bet!

We must tell the
Zebra, Lion, Leopard,
and Gator,
and not much later,
warn the snakes, frogs,
and animals down under
to get to higher ground,
because it might thunder.

No, No, not the Giraffe,
he might need to bend in half,
or else he will get a bath.

Giraffe, Giraffe, can't you see?
The rain, it's above your knee.

I am sorry for such a mess,
But I got my toe caught in
a bow and, oh, it hurt so!

If only I could break
loose and set it free.
But, what about the
rain above your knee?

We can't see to set it free.
Maybe the gator could swim and see.

Gator, Gator, Giraffe is
hurt and we are soaked.
With the tears from his
eyes we have to stroke.
Can you see to set him free?

Please, Monkey, let me be.
It is now time for my tea.
Ask the snake, frog, or
creatures in the sea.

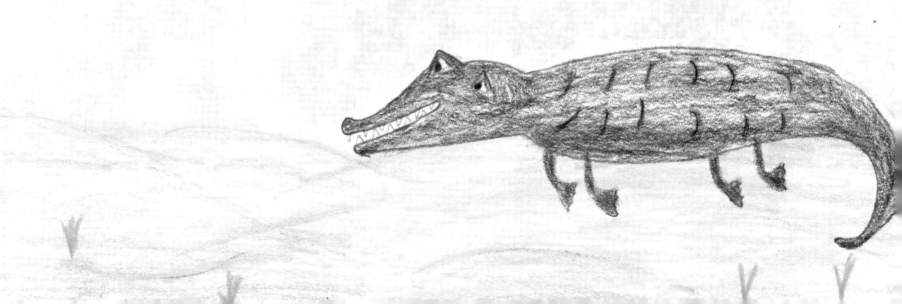

But, Mr. Gator, we can't wait any later. The Giraffe must stop crying, because his tears are making a crater.

What will you give me,
if I set him free?

I guess that will be o.k.
to have my tea today.

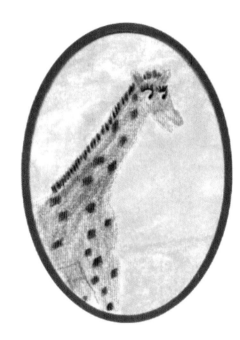

ABOUT THE AUTHOR

GLORIA MENIFIELD has spent most of her adult life around children. She has served at several elementary schools in various capacities, including kindergarten teacher.

Ms. Menifield, a native of Rosedale, Mississippi, now makes her home in Southaven, Mississippi. She is a graduate of Mississippi State University with a bachelor's degree in Sociology.

Ms. Menifield's love for children's books has led her to write and illustrate her own. When she is not creating books or assisting Desoto County residents with employment needs, Ms. Menifield enjoys spending time with her daughter Tiffany and her husband Charles.

Visit us online at www.jacksonbooks.com.